CAPTAIN PHARTO DISCIPLINES THE BRATS

A Sequel to Frank A Pellegrino's 'Phartom of the Opera - A Classic of the Gasses'

Aliceanne Pellegrino-Henricks

authorHOUSE®

AuthorHouse™
1663 Liberty Drive
Bloomington, IN 47403
www.authorhouse.com
Phone: 1-800-839-8640

First published by AuthorHouse 6/24/2010

ISBN: 978-1-4520-3440-9 (e)
ISBN: 978-1-4520-3439-3 (sc)

Library of Congress Control Number: 2010909222

Printed in the United States of America
Bloomington, Indiana

This book is printed on acid-free paper.

FOREWARD

This book is a Sequel to Frank A. Pellegrino's book,
"Phartom of the Opera - A Classic of the Gasses" written in 2004.

Frank talked about a sequel before he passed away, December 3, 2006 and many requests have
surfaced for his sequel book to be finished and published.

A monumental undertaking, his widow, Aliceanne Pellegrino-Henricks agreed to attempt
the writings and she prays that all who read the book will enjoy and laugh as hard as she did
writing it. Laughter is good for the soul and was been a wonderful therapy during her process of
grieving for her late husband.

A special Thank You to Brenda Mc Garvey, Bonnie Rogers and Ingrid Antonyshyn
They inspired this sequel with their "Stick, Bricks and Tricks" writes and bringing Granny
Aliceanne into the act of helping with a much needed disciplining.

TABLE OF CONTENTS

CHAPTER I

THE NEED FOR CAPTAIN PHARTO

AND

HIS PHARTO BLASTO TEAM

THE BRATS WITH STICKS, BRICKS AND TRICKS

I went to the woodshed to gather some firewood,
Looked out the shed window and there those brats stood.
They thought I was gathering sticks to whip their ornery butts,
They tried to lock the woodshed door and strained their guts.

I yelled and told them when I get back to house,
They better hide from me and be still as a mouse,
Would you believe those brats stole my stack of firewood?
When they were running back to the house?

They say sticks and stones will break your bones
Also words will never hurt you, but you brats better atone.
The old devil is working within those sticks,
Next thing we know you will be throwing bricks.

Now Ingrid you better set a better example for your sister,
Cause when I go after Bonnie she going to get a big blister.
Don't think you will go unnoticed or not shamed,
Cause both of you nearly killed Brenda with your big stick games.

One thing you must understand here is I don't back down,
If those sticks are not by the fireplace when I get back from town,
I found my buggy whip and your bare butts will feel its sting,
When Granny Aliceanne gets through here your butts will feel worse than a bee sting.

Brenda you behave and keep those sore legs propped up,
Sorry those brats have become so wild and corrupt.
Good thing Grandpa Franco is not here to take charge,
For he would make those brats tow the mark like an Army Sarge.

Frank A. Pellegrino

GOTTA TAME THESE BRATS

I called up my friends and said help me please,
These two brats of mine are acting like crazies.
Tried to thrash them with my buggy whip yesterday,
Now one is threatening to burn down my woodshed today.

I'm all geared up with my ammunition to take them over,
With those darn sticks I have to watch I don't fall in the clovers.
One says she can out run me and dares me to swing,
You aint seen nothing till I make their ears ring.

Make their ears ring, Froggie said don't stop there,
It is drop their pants and make them show their rears.
Plant a boomerang welp on their sorry butts,
Even if the law thinks you have gone nuts.

Mary Anne said oh Granny Aliceanne can we talk about this?
You are going to be sorry if you don't get the first lick.
I told her I tamed my two young'uns and they are still alive,
I will just put my Dodge van down the holler in over drive.

I aint stopping to think or rationalize with these two silly brats,
I've seen enough of their craziness and their squalling cat.
I called you gals up to give me a hand but I think you've gone scared,
Those two brats will hide behind you'all and think they are spared.

I believe in prayer and I believe in forgiveness too,
Neither of these two brats seem to know what is black or blue.
When I get their sorry butts over my knees, they will be begging for help to the end,
Cause I'm burning their sticks in the fireplace and branding their rear ends.

So my friends, if you want to help me or take their side in this fiasco,
It is your choice cause this Granny's got up and went needs to get up and go.
I'm a fighter not a quitter and I always win over destruction,
So these two bratty imps better not run in the wrong direction.

GRANNY'S GET NO RESPECT

I went down to the holler and stated my 1996 van,
It didn't want to start and I thought oh know they are at it again.
It finally started with a vengeance and I drove up the hill,
When a pothole my front tire hit and I thought I had it filled.

I got out and surveyed the situation with a glare of that hole,
What to my surprise were those damn sticks they thought they hid in that pot hole.
My dander was up and I knew I had to skin them alive this time,
So I went to the barn, got my razor strap and that sharp razor blind.

Oh I had a surprise for them this morning as when I left they were nasty nice,
They were snuggled on the couch by the warm fire and little crawling mice.
They didn't see or hear me come in for they were tantalizing Brenda's sweet cat,
She only wanted the mice for her dinner and those brats even stopped that.

I overheard them say they were going to put Nair on Brenda's hair to get revenge,
I knew Brenda used it all when shaving her legs last time and finished with a razor edge.
I sneaked up the steps to my bedroom and found my broken piggy bank on the bed,
I knew those brats had been in there but I'm thinking oh my gosh, Brenda's head.

With my razor strap and sharp blade, I scurried down the steps to find what I feared,
Brenda bald as an eagle and the brats asleep like they were out in the clear.
I grabbed Ingrid up by her long curly hair and I whacked off the curls one by one,
Used the cold razor on her scalp as she cried please stop are you done.

Bonnie was hiding under the credenza in the dining room watching it all in fun,
I grabbed the broom from the hallway and poked her till she cried Uncle and I gave a lunge.
I yanked her by her hair and began to scalp her like an Indian so pretty,
Ingrid cried out, I'm sorry Granny I talked Bonnie in to doing all my crazies.
Brenda said they both did this to me and I was duct taped too,
So now I have three bald Eagles looking at you.

Not only are they bald on top but their butts are a sorry sight,
I know in my heart two wrongs don't make a right.
But if I had left these two brats to continue doing all their crazies,
They will never grow up to be decent young ladies.

Frank A. Pellegrino

YOUR THINK YOU HAD THE LAST WORD

I can tell I am from a different generation than you brats,
Always thinking you know everything using sticks and bats.
You live in a fantasy world with your heads in the clouds and sky,
Never hearing or obeying your elders and always asking why.

You started out playing with sticks and playing uncouth tricks,
Then came the stumbling blocks and Brenda fell over the bricks.
You just kept doing all these bad things and blaming on each other,
You are just lucky you don't have 4 big, strong healthy brothers.

They would be kicking your butt bigger than I can or should,
I know one brother who would strangle that cat if he could.
Don't you feel bad using Nair on Brenda's hair and making her bald?
I got revenge for her by giving you a bald razor edge scald.

I don't know how much time it is going to take to make you realize,
But you can't hide from me under those wigs as I have a surprise.
You think putting ex-lax chunks in my coffee was a big joking funny hit,
Well when you locked the bathroom door, I left you a present in the floor of a big sh**.

The lane has been blacktopped so it will be icy when you try to run from me,
My horse drawn sled will capture you and I will be hands free.
Your sorry butts may be sore and red now,
But that won't stop me from using my buggy whip somehow.

You looked like bald eagles when I got though with you last night,
Now you are wearing wigs like cats and look such a scary fright.
I have decided to call in the Welfare Child Protection people to do their thing,
I know they can put you on the chain gang and I don't want to hear you complain.

If they don't take this bratty craziness out of your system soon,
Hell hath no fury cause believe me your doomed.

AINT NO RESPECT ANYMORE

Lordy, Lordy I do declare, those brats have done it again,
Think they had to have the last say before they blast off in sin.
You think you will put anything over on Captain Pharto,
He already notified Grandpa and Grandpa said to get Captain Stinko.
With Captain Stinko on the Pharto Blasto ship,
He will make you understand about this trip.
You won't get any special favors but will see and smell a lot,
One thing for sure you better eat those beans and empty the pot.

Captain Stinko talks a lot and he expects those pharts to come from you.
He tells it like it is and here is some pharts that will turn you blue.
Sometimes those pharts will be hard to tell,
What that horrible odor is you smell.
Sometimes the pharts smell so bad,
Your temper will rile and make you mad.
Sometimes the odor is like sewer fumes,
Or perhaps smell like that ten cents a gallon perfume.

If you inhale that rancid smell of sauerkraut,
Hope it don't make you puke or pass out.
Some of those pharts on board smell like rotten fish,
Wishing you had been good brats will be your number one wish.
You will wish you had been good and were not all alone,
When those pharts start smelling like strong cologne.
If you brats have pharts that smell like Chanel Number Five,
Captain Stinko says you will be lucky to come out alive.

Grandpa said heaven help you if your pharts smell like a skunk,
The buggy whip will be used if you start smelling like a drunk.
Thank God the Blasto Ship doesn't have an elevator,
Because the Blasto Ship has hippie like alligators.
If you begin to get a sulphur like smell it will be coming from your pet,
It is also a paralyzing smell you won't forget.
So Grandpa's advice to you on this rehabilitation trip in space,
Is to eat your beans, phart a lot and protect your face.

Frank A. Pellegrino

CHAPTER II

SEQUEL TO PHARTOM OF THE OPERA

A CLASSIC OF THE GASSES

PHARTO NUKES

There was an explosion in a chemical plant,
It knocked every body's gas, out of their pants.
It blasted some live sockets,
So powerful, it launched an unscheduled, flying rocket.
It flew real fast, and out of sight,
Passed the Moon, and into the night.
It landed on Mars, and turned over,
Lo and Behold, it was the 'ROVER'.
So great was the explosion, they called the Rover 'Pharto',
The second Rover landed later, called 'BLASTO'.
With the temperature, minus two below,
They were looking for good old H2o.

No sign of water or humans anywhere,
It has been said, there is no one there.
I know, there are humans there, and others,
On TV, I saw on Mars, the Wright Brothers.
There was still a Phart smell, from the Rover pair,
Such a stench, that even a politician can't bear.
They'll tell us, they couldn't find, even a rat,
No humans, no water, no life, not even a bat.

There was a secondary 'Pharts Blast',
Which made the world's skies overcast.
They all blasted 'Pharts' towards the Moon,
Hoping to land there by the noon.

More 'Pharts' and speed,
Is all they would need.
I can't believe, on Mars, there is no one,
Anything can live, under a sun.
The reason our rocket's speed is so fast,
They mix 'chemicals with pharts' that blasts and lasts.

[THIS IS THE FIRST OF MANY SHORT STORIES, IN MY NEW BOOK
'A SEQUEL TO PHARTOM OF THE OPERA - A CLASSIC OF THE GASSES]

Frank A. Pellegrino

CAPTAIN PHARTO TO THE RESCUE

There was an explosion in a chemical plant,
It knocked everybody's gas, out of their pants.
So powerful, it blasted some live sockets,
It launched an unscheduled, flying rocket.

It flew real fast, and out of sight,
Passed the Moon, and into the night.
It landed on Mars, and turned over,
Lo and Behold, it was the 'ROVER'.

So great was the explosion, they called the Rover 'Pharto'
The second Rover landed later, called 'BLASTO'.
With the temperature, minus two below,
They were looking for good old H2o.

No sign of water or humans anywhere,
It has been said, there is no one there.
I know, there are humans there, and others,
On TV, I saw on Mars, the famous Wright Brothers.

There was still a horrible Phart smell, from the Rover pair,
Such a stench, that even a politician can't bear.
They'll tell us, they couldn't find, even a rat,
No humans, no water, no life, not even a bat.

There was a secondary 'Pharts Blast',
Which made the world's skies become overcast.
They all blasted 'Pharts' towards the Moon,
Hoping to land there by the time of noon.

More 'Pharts' and more speed,
Is all they would really need.
I can't believe, on Mars, there is no one,
Because anything can live, under the sun.

The reason our rocket's speed is so fast,
They mix 'chemicals with 'pharts' that blasts and lasts.
Captain Pharto called Granny for some help with his mission
He said he needed brats, mice, rats, and pharts for emission.

Granny said you called at the right time for I can supply,
The brats are bald, the rats eat the mice but on the cat you can rely.
Just give me the nod Captain Pharto and I will line them up for you,
You might have to use my buggy whip on this mission too.

Be sure they have plenty of beans to eat and a jug of water for each,
It is going to be a long trip and I'll need lots of Pharto gas to reach.
Granny was happy as she now had those brats under the Captains control,
They can't get in trouble on this mission unless they try something too bold.

Captain Pharto is Grandpa's best friend in space,
Grandpa told Captain Pharto he could win this race.
Grandpa will sit on the moon and watch you all from afar
You will know he saw you when he pokes you with a star.

Frank A. Pellegrino

THE PHARTO SHIP CREW HAS ARRIVED

Captain Pharto learned how incorrigible these brats are to handle,
So he increased his Pharto Blasto crew to make this flight manageable.
He doesn't want to be an ogre by himself so he picked up UFO aliens to help,
Making sure he has at least 10 little green men to make buggy whip welps.

Captain Pharto and Captain Stinko hired Pharto Gasso and Captain Bruto,
They all agreed they may have to pass Mars and land on Pluto.
These brats just don't take no for an answer and keep doing stupid antics,
They are in for a big surprise with the Pharto Blasto team fanatics.

You better make sure your cohorts you conger up to blast off on this trip,
Can handle the phart odors and ex-lax and play no tricks.
For Captain Bruto is mean and he will open the doors and pitch out,
Any shenanigans from anyone he will do more than pout.

The UFO aliens on board will take care of the little green men,
You will be lucky as they prey on bratty women and sin.
The Pharto Ship has a limited number of rooms and weight,
With a crew of twenty Pharto Gasso's they will soon close the gate.

My advice to each of you brats is to heed attention,
One by one you will meet the Gasso crew and their no phart prevention.
When they say eat those beans and other gassy produce,
Better swallow fast so your pharts won't become loose.

Your behavior, which I doubt will be very disobedient as seen,
I suggest you follow directions and stop being mean.
This whole Pharto crew has been thoroughly instructed,
Not to land anywhere near home until you can be trusted.

PHARTO SHIP BLASTS OFF

Phantom Pharto checked in with Captain Pharto and said all systems are go,
He said make sure all crew is accounted for and the brats are not a no-show.
At blast off you will never hear such exploding sounds
You might think you are on and experiencing military grounds.
The Pharto crew will blast at the same time, one will go boom and another zoom.
You might think its artillery fire at lift off, but don't just assume.

You will meet a guy who thinks he is a smarty,
Because he is the biggest crew member named Mr. Pharty.
All night long, he will phart on the ships linoleum,
Bet you will think it is the cannons from Napoleon.
He eats Mexican beans, soybeans and good ole pharting beans,
Sometimes he eats too many and pharts all over his jeans.

You brats were so obnoxious and brought your ugly pets too,
Captain Bruto put you in a special cage just to protect you.
He injected the pets with special toxic gasses for the whole trip to last,
So be careful, cover your eyes when they get started passing their gas.
As you ascend into the atmosphere you will never feel secure,
But once you start repenting someday you brats may be cured.

Keep your eye on Mr. Pharty cause he is likely to explode,
Cause he blasts and pharts a lot from eating and his pants will overload.
In the next day or two he will phart a king size one,
You will know how big when he blasts the Pharto ship past the sun.
When on your way to Mars you will get to visit the Rover,
Mr. Smarty's heavy pharto blast will cause the Rover to roll over,

You will be amazed to his power as he blasted the Rover with his pharto gas,
The Rover's engines were energized and started with a big blast.
The Martians on the Rover could not stand the smell,
Like you, they believed they were headed straight to hell.
Captain Pharto said to leave you brats alone so you could be silent and bored,
You watched the Rover's powerful engines as they roared.

You noticed the Pharto ship had already ran out of toilet paper,
Now everyone on board will have to use a scraper.

Frank A. Pellegrino

JUST SO YOU KNOW

Now that you are orbiting in outer space, I thought you would like to know,
There is a lot of information that Captain Pharto and Captain Bruto have to show.
That Phartom Bomb blasts won't stop while you are on this mission with them,
You are miserable like you made Brenda and now you are paying for your sins.

Don't expect to be comfortable and you will go through a lot of tension,
Like yesterday when you blasted off you had to pay a lot of attention.
Just remember this is not the ordinary shuttle but it is a "State of the Art",
So when called on just put your behind on the canvas and phart, phart, phart!

One thing you must remember you both have an expensive king of gas,
One thing for sure it will smell but won't tarnish like brass.
Throughout you life so far, you have taken a long time to store it,
Luckily for you now, you can phart and deposit it on any planet.

Your first of your last blasts will be the moon's craters and ditches,
So release a lot so you can see the dust and black witches.
When someone in the Pharto ship lab, drops a wrench,
Watch out for the deadly smell, for it is a deadly stench.

Oh no, you brats started trouble with your pranks,
Look out for you will see the big stinks in all the tanks.
You brats are like jokesters, your mischief has escalated,
Your stench is so strong, some of the crew almost fainted.

Captain Bruto went for some extra advise and called his Aunt Emma,
She said the best advice she knew was to give you brats a cold enema.
While waiting for the water to get cold, there was found a big mistake,
You two blasted out some windows that no one else could break.

Your horrible blast reached my old country farm,
Thank God it did no harm, by missing my new barn.
They said not even a large cork could stop your deadly blast,
Now your really in trouble with the Captain Bruto who hopes this won't last.

Captain Pharto said not even his armored car,
Coming so fast, couldn't be picked up by his radar,
After all your blasto damage, there was even mountain erosion,
Your deadly pharts finally dropped out into the ocean.

You made history with your Pharto bombs as they had to be weighed on the scales,
Now I am making profits off you brats with all the gas masks that went up for sale.
As for your ugly pets, you better keep a strong eye on them now,
The Pharto crew is not happy with them and will do away with them somehow.

CAPTAIN PHARTO ABANDONS THE GRAND CANYON

Mr. Pharto a crewman won a very big contest,
You know it was about 'who could phart the best'.
He pharted with the help of the brats through a big fish tank,
A winner they made him and he pharted all the way to the bank.

Mr. Pharto had experimented with an unknown gas,
At times the brats said it sounded a lot like jazz.
Other times the pharts created cloudy skies,
The brats kept saying hope nobody dies.

With all these loud and exploding blasts,
The brats thought what good are these gas masks?
The next big blast could knock Planets out of line,
And for the most part, the population would decline.

Mr. Pharto put his special formula on a teaspoon,
Just enough formula to take a rocket to the dark side of the moon.
On the side of the moon, you could see a crowd of witches,
The brats heard the blasts and saw the witches crawl out of the ditches.

The witches tried to attack the rocket,
But the brats and Mr. Pharto's pharts buried their sockets.
Mr Pharto escaped, left the brats behind as he flew to Mars,
A film of this showed oil on the tires of the Rover cars.

The film also showed that the news did falter,
They did not tell the crew and people that there is water.
A lesson the brats learned that lying is worse than a curse,
Because there is life on every planet in the Universe.

Mr. Pharto didn't want to phart as they orbited over New York,
So he made sure the brats and himself were wearing a big cork.
The brats thought it was funny when Mr. Pharto pharted,
Because they realized some people were politely departed.

The brats became scared and didn't know what to do at this point,
They looked around to see if Mr. Pharto was smoking a joint.
Mr. Pharto said the cork source gas, etc., he would have to abandon,
So he dumped everything into the Grand Canyon.

Frank A. Pellegrino

CAPTAIN PHARTO STRIKES AGAIN

He came with a blast of very hot air,
He made the trees go instantly bare.
The stench he blasted had agonizing fumes,
It was like some had eaten a lot of boiled prunes.

The stench was enough to make one gag and be sad,
It appeared to come from the direction of a scientific lab.
You see they were experimenting with garlic, onion and a hot pepper mix,
They even added a special gas for the brats to get some big kicks.

Captain Pharto mixed all of it and out came the big sparks,
An explosion happened with Pharto Blasto Pharts.
You could tell it went easily through the wall,
The explosion rolled up the highway like a ball.

They were hoping to create more and more power,
So they had added to the mixture some cauliflower.
Just when things began to go sour,
It started bubbling, and went on hour after hour.

You see this is how with the two brats it all started,
They caused big Pharto, oh how he pharted!
They were so powerful, when this mix released,
The brats said we are not safe, nor is man or beast.

This mixture wound up in a trench over in Mars,
Landed miraculously on the Rover cars.
Somehow it ricocheted and came back to Earth,
Even had a box full of the Mar's surf.

Captain Pharto thought he had made another mixture,
So he pharted and blew everyone but the brats out of the picture.
Captain Pharto then went and sat on the toilet,
He laughed and laughed and began to enjoy it.

The brats were nervous and thought oh my what is next,
This experiment must have failed and wondered what would have been best.
They knew this was a dangerous experiment that had failed,
Captain Pharto told them the crew was sentenced to a trip to Mars by Air Mail.

CHAPTER III

FIRST TEN TRIPS OF THE MISSION

CAPTAIN PHARTO LAUGHING GAS

The brats heard boom, rip, woosh, and then a crash,
Captain Pharto said it was a new rocket named "Pharto-Blast".
It is the biggest rocket since the world began,
Also the most powerful rocket ever known to man.
Captain Pharto said we got it ready to be loaded,
The brats go in and the engine exploded.

They all left the field at once,
They did not have time to even eat lunch.
Next they landed on a sandy range,
The brats said everything looked strange.
They saw two-headed geese on the loose,
Also two-headed cows and lordy a two-headed moose.

The brats said oh we know we are in trouble,
They thought for sure they were seeing double.
One brat said she was seeing everything upside down,
The other one saw double even the whole town.
They were given smelling salts up their nose,
Then they felt water on their clothes.

One said she felt like her brain had expanded,
At the same time she found out they had landed.
The other brat said her head felt hurt,
Because the rocket air conditioning didn't work.
This all happened because of the Pharto-gasses,
The stench just lasted, lasted and lasted.

Captain Pharto was given a patent from Uncle Sam,
Without Pharto gas he won't get into a jam.
Pharto Gas has changed the world,
Even made the brats hair pieces curl.
Pharto Gas has been highly admired,
But now it is about time for Pharto to retire.

Frank A. Pellegrino

THE PYRAMID EXPEDITION

What you will like here the most,
Is all the things you will be experiencing on the coast.
Captain Pharto has assigned you to work with the Marines,
You will have special chores on special submarines.
He assigned you brats to one called the "Master Blaster",
When the crew here pharts, it will go faster and faster.

When you all phart at the same time,
The crew will stop the submarine on a dime.
Now don't out do yourself when you find yourself on shore,
Don't try to shake yourself when walking out the door.
You will be sitting on rocks and you will see many mermaids,
Captain Pharto will introduce you to one named "Gasso-Maid".

Gasso-Maid will show you where they live and take you under the sea,
You can be sure you won't see any He's but plenty of She's.
The She's reproduce by lifting their legs,
Be kind to them as they gently lay their eggs.
The mermaids have a submarine of their own,
Guess what, it is powered when pharto gas is blown.

You brats must hop in and go with them on patrol,
Hop in and out of the water as things get out of control.
You will think you are truly dead,
When you speed towards the sun ahead.
You brats will totally flip your lid,
When you spot those big Pyramids.

Your eyes will burn and then you will blink,
Look out you are going to see the famous Phinx.
Next you will see the Tomb of Cheaps,
Even go with tourists on the hot spots very deep.
When on this trip if you run out of fuel, you will be put in a cell,
How long you will be there no one can tell.

Somehow you will be rescued by the "Master Blaster",
You will speed away, faster and faster.
Doctors checking you out said you had too much gas,
Hot Chili Peppers was blamed for the giant blast.

MEET CAPTAIN BEANO

Pharto-Beano came flying in at a fantastic speed,
No one anywhere on Earth could exceed.
In a short time you will all speed by Venus and Mars,
You brats will fly by the Moon, the Sun and the farthest Stars.
What the brats did not know about was Pharto-Beano's gas,
No one could ever beat this kind of gas 'passed'.

The entire crew of ten, the brats and Pharto-Beano mixed all together,
A formula they could fly the Universe forever.
All they had to do was blast away.
Good-bye Jack they were on their way.
The mixture of super gas broke the weather stagnation,
This was so bad it boggled the crew and brats imagination.

They flew to all the craters of the moon,
They flew to Uranus, to the Milky Way and even Neptune.
Lo and behold, they crashed on one side of the Planet Zone,
It was so dark the brats began to cry and were feeling very alone.
All of a sudden out of nowhere, they saw big fiery eyes,
Followed by 'hey brats" how are you guys"?

You see they were lost pilots from Earth,
They came from an area that had a high rated and mixed birth.
They said they were half Australian,
Also they were lovers, because the other half of them was Italian.
The pilots and crew got together and fixed the Pharto-Beano vehicle,
This is how Pharto-Beano got out of this pickle.

Once they reached Italy they were able to play some bocce,
You all listened to the Operetta of Pegliacci.
All of a sudden the crew realized, everyone needed to poop,
As fast as they could, they ran to the rocket, boy did they scoot.
They all came back to their planet home stinky but silent,
Now you brats will have to wait for the Captain's next assignment.

Frank A. Pellegrino

PHARTO SENIOR

Pharto Senior didn't know with the brats what he would face,
The brats were in the jail cell for twelve hours in dark space.
The giant rocket now had a crew of thirteen,
Pharto Senior found a planet on the other side of the moon, called Obscene.

Pharto Senior and his crew pharted all the way there,
They flew speeds no one else would even dare.
They landed the rocket with the nose to the ground,
They saw surrounding them one-eyed monsters all around.

These monsters had two lights on their heads,
One light was green and the other one was red.
They seemed to have a block in their mentality,
Surprisingly, it was only mental telepathy.

The leader had a banana shaped nose,
Lordy they had big feet and 8 toes.
The crew and the brats thought they were having a nightmare,
They soon realized they were real but quite rare.

The monster's mates wore skirts and their noses leaked,
They were ugly as sin with eagle shaped beaks.
The crew and the brats jumped into the rocket, ate beans and a wiener,
Then they pharted together in the rocket for Pharto Senior.

Their fuel was a mixture of turpentine and sulphur,
Also bear poop, explosives and even skunk fur.
They landed on an unknown Planet, called Pearl Island,
The brats found on the ground, large one-foot diamonds.

The brats loaded their bags with their precious find,
But they all had to leave their old pharts behind.
They pharted their way back to the U.S.A.,
Our government listened to what they had to say.

Their pay was doubled and it was suggested for retirement,
There would be no more adventure or new assignment.
Pharto Senior was one of those thirteen men,
Captain Pharto was left and said you brats will be taking this trip again.

THE HULLACINATING CREW

Uncle Sam sent out a new rocket called Pharto Niagara,
With an unheard speed, it was boosted by Viagra.
The crew had a mile long smile,
The brats said sometimes they acted senile.
Especially when the crew was ready to start,
They would fog the windows with their pharts.

The rocket orders came over their cell phones,
They were to land on the Australian Zone.
Australia had ordered cactobastos beetles,
So they could control the prickly pears with needles.
The crew had done this before more and more,
They had done this during the first Iraq War.

This is why Saddam Hussein had holes in his kisser,
Now wasn't that a pharty pisser?
The crew soon found the Viagra on their deck,
They overdosed and almost became a wreck.
The prickly pears started to act funny,
Their prickly needles prevented love with their honey.

When they woke up the next morning,
They had to leave even though it was storming.
The crew pharted their way on to Mars,
They were happy they had brought with them their guitars.
When they woke up, all the inhabitants,
They all had left in a big trance.

The brats and crew noticed the cactobastos beetles did not work,
More and more of them came out of the dirt.
The crew and brats pharted all the way to the Niagara base,
Their colors changed to purple in their face.
They were all happy and each congratulating,
Only to find out they were all hallucinating.

… Captain Pharto is upset so beware …

Frank A. Pellegrino

CRYSTALS NEEDED FOR DEFENSE

Pharto-Phart-Bean was lost in the ocean,
Causing a lot of sorrow and commotion.
Uncle Sam had just made a new one-celled Pharto Flame,
The brats jumped for joy and thought this is a new ball game.

To get started here, the crew pharted together,
They threw crystals in the clouds to change the weather.
Throwing them into the clouds caused the weather to bring rain,
Tough on the older crew and caused them arthritic pain.

The crystals also caused some of the crew and the brats to lose their hair,
While this was being experimented, it brought on some good warfare.
Less crystals, Captain Pharto said would not work,
But it was good for the farmers here on Earth.

Pharto Flame flew farther into space,
Into the darkness he flew at a faster pace.
They landed on a planet that looked like a jungle,
The name of this planet was "Uncle".

The brats and crew marched by the moldy trees,
In marshy waters that was up to their knees.
Two crew members fell in the wet rubble,
While under the water they pharted bubbles.

The crew and brats heard a loud eerie sound,
It sounded like Aliens were all around.
Those aliens were wild and uncivilized,
You could tell it when you looked into their eyes.

The aliens could not take the bright sun,
They covered up their eyes, one by one.
Pharto-Phart Flame made the aliens run,
The crew and brats were now having lots of fun.

They began to throw crystals into the sky,
One by one, the aliens began to die.
Seems the experimental crystals were a success,
Another priority in defense of the U.S.

THE BRATS NIGHTMARISH DREAM

The brats were hearing all kinds of exploding sounds,
Like they were in the military on experimental grounds.
Nearby, they were seeing old Napoleon cannons,
They were pouring secret fuel in the cannons by the gallons.
Pharto Busto said let's all phart at the same time,
Be sure to put on your safety glasses so you won't go blind.

So together with the brats the whole crew pharted,
All their gas from their pants soon departed.
The Napoleon cannons rolled down the hill,
Before their eyes, the cannon blew up the old sawmill.
When Pharto Busto got over heated,
The brats and crew got back in the rocket and repeated.

They decided to fly to another planet called Phart-It,
With such speeds, they flew like big pharting bullets.
When they landed, they saw men in military clothes,
Standing at attention were silver-colored UFOs.
They said they were there to explore,
Their leaders said they wanted more and more.

They even said they were prisoners of war,
So Pharto-Busto's began to roar.
The crew counted twenty-five pinheads,
They were all left behind without any heads.
Pharto Busto rocket, shaped like a pen,
Had again, done it up well and again.

Then, when the vegetables turned into vegetable human beings,
The crew and the brats could not believe what they were seeing.
The crew was told these pinheads never left their area,
This almost caused a loud hysteria.
They were given secret pills in their coffee and cream,
Now you know what caused their nightmarish dream.

Frank A. Pellegrino

LOST IN SPACE FOR A TIME

The bell struck twelve and it was now midnight,
No one, not even the devil was in sight.
Lo and behold there came a deafening loud blast,
Here came a lost Pharto Blasto from the past.
Pharto Blasto was glad to be home, there were lots of smiles,
They had traveled through the universe ten thousand miles.
The brats said OMG there is a crew of fifty plus
Would you believe, it was the size of a city bus.

They all pharted and yes at the same time,
Glass broke in pieces smaller than a dime.
The next flight would require a lot of new fuel,
This fuel so powerful you would call it a new tool.
This fuel could penetrate almost anything,
Leaving behind a mile-long smoke ring.
This powerful fuel was a mixture of high octane gas,
It contained sulphur, cabbage, hot peppers and crab grass.

One of the worse stinko's was FAVA beans,
It also contained leftover hash from New Orleans.
They were prepared to leave at dawns first light,
Ignited by two sticks of dynamite.
The crew circled the Earth in a tenth of an hour,
They reached an unknown Planet, called Tower.
Here on this Planet they found large purple ants,
Also four footed talking female plants.

The crew wanted to pot them and place them near their bunks,
But the plants and their wives would talk too much.
So the crew left and flew past the stars,
They landed on their favorite Planet, Mars.
The stinko gasses and the windows corroded,
When they opened the window, Pharto Blasto exploded.
Now they are lost in time and space forever,
The brats wondered if they would be back or perhaps never.

PHARTO BEANO MEETS PHARTO ZOO

It seems a meteor was about to crash,
The U.S. sent out a rocket called Pharto Gas.
It was to meet up with Pharto It,
Hoping to see if it would split.
No one knew where this rocket had gone,
Pharto Beans thought it had landed in Oregon.

They thought they saw something on the long trail,
Would you believe it was Big Foot without a tail?
They captured them and put them on a scale,
They were too big to put them in jail.
Pharto Gas, gassed them up full,
Away from Earth gravity did pull.

They reached a Planet called Zeno.
There they ate a lot of gassy beano.
What was so surprising is there were no sounds,
They spoke, but could not hear they had been found.
They saw mountains, but they were bare,
They even saw people and animals that had no hair.

The brats were shocked they could not hear anything,
They could not even hear a bird sing.
They were so sick and showed lots of emotion,
Once they were pulled out of the ocean.
All of a sudden to the brats surprise, they could once again hear,
Their ears and eyes became quite clear.

Because the Pharto-Gas was now overloaded,
It crashed in the ocean and exploded.
The crew thought they had hit the dirt,
But they hit the nearest Planet to Earth.
The full story of Pharto Zoo was never fully understood,
Because this episode was not filmed in Hollywood.

Frank A. Pellegrino

A FRIEND IN AUSTRALIA

The pilots name is Pharto-Nuke,
The co-pilots name is Pharto-Luke.
There was nothing they could not sustain,
Believe me they had ice in their veins.
Their mission was the Australian country,
It was a rest area as far as anyone could see.

The brats noticed a farm that was full of kangaroos,
Instead of one neck and head, the kangaroos had two.
Pharto Nuke gave the kangaroos pharto gas,
Oh my you could hear powerful gas pass.
What the brats saw next was quite a strange thing,
Those weird kangaroos began sprouting wings.

From here on in there were no more kangaroos hopping.
So the brats and their women friends took the children shopping.
The women put their children in their pouches,
Their babies slept like those pouches were couches.
The crew gave Pharto Gas to the ostriches,
They mated them with the kangaroos and dressed them in britches.

The hybrid births looked like Satan,
The other half of them looked like Bin-Laden.
The co-pilots overdosed them and soon after killed them,
The pilots buried them and hoped they would never see them again.
Many moons and Pharto gas have been passed,
Somehow the brats and crew were accidentally gassed.

They were sent back to a U.S. military hospital base,
Because our situation was a very bad case.
They were to be treated as very serious,
Because they were seriously very delirious.
The crew and brats were all in a rage,
They were treated as loonies and put in a gas-free cage.

CHAPTER IV

THE BRATS WITH CAPTAIN PHARTO

WATER DISCOVERED ON MARS –PLUS ALIENS

Pharty Phart Flame was ready for other adventures,
At speeds enough to vibrate everyone's dentures.
They flew from Pluto, Uranus and then to Mars,
A giant planet so bare one could see ancient scars.
The long adventure was abruptly over,
When the crew discovered the American Rover.

One man and each crew got in and went for a ride,
They wanted to see what was on the other side.
Lo and Behold with a camera in motion,
The crew saw clearly a gigantic ocean.
Scientists had predicted water would be found there,
What they didn't expect to find was …. BEER.

You see there are no Planets dying of thirst,
Because God provided life all over his Universe.
The crew thought the scientists were somewhat insane,
Or perhaps they were born short of brains.
Captain Pharty Phart Flame predicted water would be found on Mars real soon,
But he also wanted to know what was on the dark side of the moon.

He said if we have fifty or a hundred of Pharty Phart Flames,
Soon we can take tourists there with two continuous lanes.
The Rover drivers saw alien creatures,
They had protruding eyeballs and primitive features.
Protruding from their head was a single antenna,
Flashing red eyes like embers from Mt. Etna.

One fierce look the brats saw from their eyes,
They wondered if they would make the crew paralyzed.
The crew leader ordered for every one to pull their pants down,
They were to all phart on them with 'pharts brown'.
The aliens soon died from suffocation,
This made their brains go on vacation.

The Pharty Phart Flame crew took off at a high speed,
A speed no one could ever exceed.
There is more adventure where all this came from
The Captain and brats are waiting for another exciting one.
Ingrid told Bonnie that she was missing their friend Brenda today.
She was going to ask Captain Pharto to pick up Brenda someway.

Frank A. Pellegrino

PEACEFUL PHART LAND ISLAND

One of the twenty-crew members was playing a banjo,
So orders were given to get on the rocket called Pharto Banjo.
To fly straight to the Earth and pickup Brenda at the borders,
Until further notice the crew will fly under sealed orders.
They saw something that looked like 4 dogs a thousand feet below,
It was Captain Pharto with Brenda, her four dogs standing with a huge UFO.

The UFO doors opened up like an eye socket,
Magnetically they drew in the Pharto Banjo rocket.
They said they were from Phart Land Island,'
They would be happy to guide them wherever they wished to land.
They said this is their ancient place of birth,
It was on a beautiful planet called Blue Earth.

All the people on Blue Earth wanted out,
They had too much sickness like arthritis and gout.
To help them heal their miserable condition of sinus,
They wanted to find a cure in Uranus.
They finally landed and were amazed what they saw,
Aliens with protruding teeth from their jaws.

Captain Pharto told the brats and Brenda this is peaceful planet with no crimes,
He wanted them to know it was way ahead of their time.
He said they did not have or live sinful lives,
They all were married here and were husband and wives.
They believe in doing no one any harm,
But guilty brats with sticks, bricks and tricks would be sent to a funny farm.

They loaded the Pharto Banjo with a big food supply,
They ate real food and began to feel sick, but couldn't understand why.
So the Pharto Banjo crew began to phart meatball pharts,
These pharts were extreme and really defensive arts.
If you brats think this episode is hard to swallow,
Wait until you experience the next episode to follow.

SHORT TRIP TO THE MOON

Pharto Bomb was flying the skies to fame,
His crew knew it was a dangerous game.
They saw UFO's in the chilly air,
To approach them, they really didn't care.
The UFO's were headed for the planet Neptune,
While Pharto Bomb decided to head straight to the Moon.

They landed in a field of corn and grapevines,
These grapevines could produce great wines.
They all, brats included drank old wine and ate Pharto Beans,
They all pharted through their smelly jeans.
They ate so much they came apart at the seams,
Aliens looked at them and said are they human beings.

The aliens remembered Niagara Falls, U.S.A.,
They remembered a man visiting two years ago today.
His name was Frank and from the beautiful Niagara Falls,
They had been stuck there when their rocket stalled.
They had been offered, but refused to go back on Pharto Bombs return,
Love and Peace is better here and something your brats need to learn.

So Pharto Bomb and his crew drank all their booze,
Even drank milk, from the milking cow, Mooze.
The brats were shocked when they saw two-headed cows with triple nipples,
Also monkeys and baboons playing with their fiddles.
Soon they realized it had to be the crazy old wine they had drank,
So the brats put the rest in the Pharto Bomb rocket tank.

Away they flew hoping to land in the states,
With all the wine and the cows in their crates.
They had made new secret energy fuel again,
Didn't land in the states, but saw new training Pharto crew men.
The next adventure will probably be better,
Who knows they might be in outer space forever.

Frank A. Pellegrino

LIFE ON THE MEDITERRANEAN SEA

Pharto Stinko's maiden voyage is headed to the Ozone,
This fantastic rocket speeding into the unknown.
They landed on a small Planet called "Beans",
It was so pretty more beautiful than any dreams.
The brats said this is like a fairy land,
With games, and a marching band.

They could see different species of aliens,
There were also extremely beautiful maidens.
There were live fish walking on the ground,
Some were five feet tall making pharting sounds.
In a corner they saw a family of Big-Foot,
Eating away apples, carrots and roots.

Pharto and crew had a real good time,
But time to phart their way into the sunshine.
They went to a Planet called Zone,
The brats said its too cold and we are all alone.
They soon found some people on a farm,
One by one they were taken to the barn by their arm.

They were shown cattle with two heads and tails,
Triple shells housing triple snails.
The brats couldn't believe any of this and called them liars,
But they proved they could reproduce aliens in a matter of hours.
Pharto Stinko joined in the fun,
Said he produced twenty-four sons.

The crew and brats pharted their way out like flashing guns,
Leaving behind their alien sons.
They crashed into the Mediterranean Sea,
Sunk too deep to be rescued and set free.
Pharto Stinko phoned into his base in Dallas,
Told them they were living in Charlie Tuna's palace.

Each crew member had a mate, so they each called their wife,
Now they will enjoy peace, no noises, no war and a perfect life.
So far Pharto Stinko was the last of high technology,
He told his crew and the brats to enjoy life here and accept my apology.

PHARTO THE WORLD TRAVELER

It will make you ache and chill to your bones,
If you drive by or pass into the Pharto Zones.
The Pharto Gas is a secret weapon,
It is utilized by Captain Pharto's rocket, the size of a Zeplin.
Pharto was so intelligent and he could envision,
Why he was being sent on this special mission.
Uncle Sam sent Pharto to the Russian Square,
They seemed to be having an over population of bears.

Pharto pharted and somehow the bears became few,
The air ciculated and the Russian people were rescued.
The Pharto secret fuel and Pharto had worked once again,
Russia's Prime Minister placed a medal on him.
After this calling, Pharto was sent to the Middle East,
Pharto and his crew were called to capture Bin-Laden, the beast.
A large reward was placed on the crew's head,
The reward won't be paid if Bin-Laden is dead.

The brats told Captain Pharto that they were scared,
But Captain Pharto told them if they were good they would be spared.
Pharto the Third and his pharting crew
Oh my what a stench when they pharted together, Phew!
The brats said these were so powerful from this crews blast,
It even changed the weather's forecast.
The pharts created an awful situation,
The pharts even knocked out the rocket's communication.

The crew got off course and lost ending up at the North Pole,
They were all pharting, stinking and looked like lost souls.
The rocket plunged into the Arctic,
The whole crew survived by eating lots of garlic.
When the rescuers came they were given water in cycles,
The brats and crew were so cold and were frozen like icicles.
The crew and brats disappeared into the night,
But they had enjoyed seeing the 'Northern Lights".

Frank A. Pellegrino

PHARTO FOUR ADVENTURE

Pharto with the brats wanted revenge,
They flew in Pharto Four to Stonehenge.
They all thought they might find bones,
Looking under the huge Stonehenge stones.

As part of their discipline the brats were digging and didn't know,
The green aliens were there to build a big U.F.O.
Those aliens told them they had been there for five thousand years,
The aliens remembered seeing cave men hunting with spears.

From the early life of this Earth planet,
They all knew they had to stay and save it.
After the crew thought about it and with speculation,
The all pharted and flew across this great nation.

Once in France, the crew pharted with a horrible stench,
The stench mummified the wine, drinking French.
One member of the crew was out of place,
The secret fuel blew him into outer space.

Pharto saw a speeding Meteor,
Swinging wildly the needle on his meter.
Pharto raced all the way to an Island near the U.S.A.,
They had all had enough for this adventure today.

LOST IN SPACE JUST FOR NOW

Oh no, the brats said, here comes Pharto 5 again,
We thought he was out of our lives and now he has a crew of ten.
Pharto 5 raced through the race track,
What a sight as he roared and flipped on contact.
This was the crew's luckiest day,
As they pharted and blasted away.

They flew away from our borders,
Pharting away under sealed traveling orders.
The orders were read by Captain Bruto,
They were on track traveling to Pluto.
When the crew of ten pharting ceased,
Their incredible speed decreased.

A most beautiful live creation,
Pharto's crew detected radiation.
Pluto people came to greet the crew,
They introduced themselves as Pharto Overdue.
The Pharto Overdue pulled a stun gun,
The Pharto crew were not about to run.

They all pharted a powerful red dye,
The Pluto natives were left to die.
Pharto number 5 lived to survive,
He came back to the U.S.A, very much alive.
They broke open an enormous size door,
Inside was a large UFO on the floor.

They got in and visited all the stars,
Finally they raced towards the Planet Mars.
In was quiet and peaceful in the air,
There were purple people everywhere.
They were going to report to Earth about this race,
On the way back Pharto 5 was lost in space.

Frank A. Pellegrino

PHARTO SIX DREAM

In the last episode Pharto 5 was lost in space,
It wasn't hard for him to be replaced.
Pharto 6 was carrying a heavy load,
No one really knew it was about to explode.
They were all together and bent over and pharted,
They blasted off vibrating as they departed.

They flew farther and farther into the Ozone,
Into a Planet that was a solidly frozen zone.
They even saw a Planet that was as small as a dot,
Reaching it they found it was extremely hot.
People there poured out their charm,
They wanted to show them their farm.

You won't believe this, but they had six feet acorns,
They even had twenty feet high sweet corn.
They had sunflowers round as a car wheel,
There were four big seeds enough for a meal.
Vegetables big enough to feed all of the Earth,
The crew took home samples of this dirt.

Pharto 6 and his crew pharted to a Planet called Bridget,
Surprise, Surprise said the brats, it looks like a Planet of Midgets.
They showed them a tunnel that went underground,
They found UFO's ready to take off without making a sound.
The Pharto 6 crew pharted and pharted around,
The brats said they are pharting, pound by pound and more pound.

Their combined pharts created a huge explosion,
Which caused landslides and a mountain erosion.
The heat was so intense they blew out the window glass,
Slowly but slowly it let out the pharto gas.
Pharto 6 woke up and this story they could not explain,
Because Captain Pharto said they were over dosed with cocaine.

PHARTO SEVEN FROM HEAVEN

The brats told Captain Pharto they saw a monster vehicle coming from the heavens,
Captain Pharto said it could be Pharto 7 with his useless crew of seven.
They saw their powerful gas fumes in the skies,
Very soon the powerful gas was penetrating the brats eyes.
Pharto Blasto decided to send out a scout,
Soon after Pharto Blasto himself stepped out.

Although Captain Pharto had not planned it,
They were sent to a secret planet.
They met people that pretty much looked like we do,
Except their skin was of a royal blue.
Women here were controlled with ball and chain,
The brats were scared and wondered if they were in any pain.

The chains were secured around their legs,
Each woman was carrying a large bag.
They chased Pharto7 into the rocket den,
Explaining to the brats they have no men.
The running crew stopped on a dime,
After all they had plenty of time.

Their eggs would hatch almost every day,
All their men were on an adventure far away.
Pharto 7 told the brats this is hard to believe,
He told the brats to get ready so they could leave.
Pharto 7 and his crew of 7 pharted altogether,
They breathe a sigh and they all felt better.

Again the crew pharted all at once
Landed in Washington bounce after bounce.
They made an agreement and then arranged,
Two eggs for Hollywood left wingers in the exchange.
Captain Pharto told the brats that secret Planet was an intelligent planet,
They all clapped and sighed for the rejection of the Jackson, Janet.

Frank A. Pellegrino

PHARTO EIGHT AND THE TIME MACHINE

Pharto 8 was involved in a world race,
He was competing with others in outer space.
For a moment they appeared behind,
Pharto 8 Commander said let us put together all our behinds.
At the count of three let's all phart away,
They did, but didn't expect to pass the Milky Way.

The pharts so powerful that Pharto 8 reached Venus,
They said their people had seen us.
They gave us their concoction to eat,
It was tasty but smelled like sheep.
They said it would put hair on their chest,
Except for the bald ones, it would make a good bird's nest.

The brats holding their nose said a skunk would smell better,
Captain Pharto said do you want to put the skunk on a tester?
The women aliens all carried witches brooms,
They were ready to go with Pharto 8 but there was no room.
In the middle and still of the night,
Pharto 8 with his crew and brats snuck out without fright.

They all began pharting at the scene,
They sped right smack into the Time Machine.
The Time Machine brought them to pre-cave men time,
They stopped when they became small as a dime.
They started pharting again, one by one,
Away they flew, away past the sun.

They landed on a Planet called Earth,
This is how they came to a re-birth.
This was actually a military experiment,
Captain Pharto told the brats it was a successful experience.
Now the public and the brat's friends can sign up and get ready to go,
Secret name and number is PHARTO 8 UFO.

CHAPTER V

TRIPS THROUGH THE UNIVERSE

WITH THE ALIENS

PHARTO NINE EXPEDITIONS

They were on an adventurous trip on the rocket Pharto Nine,
They were on a secret mission and one of a special kind.
They had been in cold, hot and other kinds of turf,
They had gone to almost everywhere on Earth.
They had to fly through terrible and all kinds of weather,
So Captain Pharto standing side by side got us all together.

All together now, we all pharted,
This how we all usually get started.
Up through the chilling ozone,
They all felt their aching bones.
We circled back and landed in the Earth's Hallow,
It was so cold the brats and crew could hardly swallow.

They saw some vehicles with a shining glow,
There were men nine feet tall standing by their UFO.
They said they could quickly release,
The UFO's to fight against wars and help make peace.
They had been there for years and years,
They told Captain Pharto his crew shouldn't have any fears.

The Pharto 9 crew's gas grew and grew,
Once they pharted together, they flew and flew.
They flew through the skies and black holes,
Flew back again to Earth again then on to the North and South Poles.
They made a quick change in flight with a pharting zoom,
Very quickly they were landing on the moon.

The brats and the crew walked into a big hole in the ground,
Inside the hole they all heard an eerie sound.
Captain Pharto said they were making a world peace date,
The brats said they saw at the head of the table, the President of the United States.
Upon the advice of the President and his orders,
They opened up once more all our borders.

Bin-Laden they say can no longer function,
Now the U.S.A. should capture him and all his mass weapons of destruction.
This scared Pharto 9 and he got ready to move,
The crew got together and pharted from their grooves.
They moved at high speeds into the night,
Straight for the sun's rays and out of sight.

Frank A. Pellegrino

PHARTOTEN AND HIS SHORT ADVENTURE

Pharto 10's pharto gas just blows and blows,
The pharto gas finds it way as it flows and flows.
The pharto gas blasts its way from the hose,
It irritates and swells the brats big nose.
This pharto gas is ten times stronger,
Somehow it lasts longer and longer.

This is the same power that sent up the Rover,
Then they set the Rover up on rollers.
This is why Captain Pharto calls them the Pharto Ten,
Pharto Ten has a pharty crew of ten men.
On the way to Neptune in outer space,
The brats saw aliens and the crew gave them a chase.

These aliens had acorn shaped heads,
Pharto 10 radioed Pharty Gas ahead.
They said Neptune had no population,
They soon found out that was an exaggeration.
When they landed in a big hurry,
The big stinko caused a fury.

The Pharto crew and brats got out of their seats,
They found female creatures with four feet.
The brats noticed they had four big hands,
Which came in handy when they played in their band.
It wasn't long till the male aliens came,
They tried to set Pharto 10 in flames.

It didn't seem to make any sense,
So the Pharto crew got together in defense.
They pharted their gas right up in the alien faces,
All that was left of them was their shoelaces.
The Pharto 10 crew flew back to the U.S.A.,
Caging the brats while waiting for another exciting day.

QUICK TRIP TO THE MOON

Captain Pharto said I was born with an antenna in my head,
He came from a far away planet someone said.
Captain Pharto was told when he was about seven,
He had come from far away in Heaven.
When he was old enough he joined a Pharto crew,
This crew taught him more than he ever knew.

He told the brats he was taught how to blast out his gas,
How to make a stink that would last and last.
On the moon they heard a blast in a crater,
He said we can match our Pharto gas and ours will be greater.
The Pharto gas created a thick strong storm,
When the gas cleared they saw some human forms.

These humans had large heads and only one eye,
They had large wings so they could fly.
These humans brought out some trays filled with food,
The food relaxed them and put them in a good mood.
When the crew woke up they had a giant hangover,
The brats said they had a dream that they were driving the Land Rover.

They were all so ashamed for getting so drunk,
Captain Pharto told them once home they could join the monks.
The crew tried to shake it off but couldn't think,
The crew and brats all agreed they needed a shrink.
Captain Pharto said he hoped they had learned their lesson,
He then went to sleep without answering any of their questions.

He said the next time we go on another Pharto trip,
Together the crew and brats would let it rip, rip, rip.
All the plant life was dead and decayed,
Because all day long the brats and crew sprayed and sprayed.
Captain Pharto said until the next trip I'm living a normal life,
After this obnoxious trip I'm going home to be with my wife.

Frank A. Pellegrino

THE ABORTED PHARTO TRIP

THE Pharto Gaso told the brats he was near death,
When the gasso crew cut out his breath.
He was sitting on the rocket's floor,
When the crew pharted together they blew out the door.
They quickly glided on to Venus,
They noticed the aliens there were super genius.

Pharto Gaso was soon healed and would recover,
Because soon he was to meet one love sick brat for his lover.
They would have a farm with two headed cows,
Flying overhead would be a group of giant owls.
They would put some of the owls in their rocket,
The brats put giant seeds in their pockets.

The crew pharted together so they could get started,
Pharto Gaso hit their eyes by mistake and it smarted.
They all drank the pharto gas from a glass,
Very soon they all pharted that special gas.
The speed was not in full swing,
It proved to be faster than anything.

They flew around the moon and the sun,
They pharted around the sun and the brats said this is a lot of fun.
They were eating a lot of their magic mushrooms,
Even made the brats see witches on their brooms.
Now the crew didn't know what to do,
So they gathered close together and let out a few.

Finally they blasted away out into the Heavens,
Never to return till the year two thousand eleven.
The brats prayed and hoped that someone will come here,
For fear they would blow up everything in the atmosphere.
As sure as an aching back or tooth,
This episode is nothing but the honest truth.

PHARTO THIRTEEN WANTED OUT

Pharto Thirteen just couldn't help himself,
As he pharted in the face of his friend, an Elf.
Poor Elf couldn't get out of the way in time,
Being in the way was his only crime.
The Pharto crews got together and pharted,
But the little Elf was to be outsmarted.

When the crew was through, the Elf aimed at Pharto 13 eyes,
He hit the bull's eye and stunk enough to make Pharto 13 cry.
Next they sped to the Planet of Caves,
Here they met a guard and all his slaves.
One of the slaves fell in love with Pharto 13,
But Pharto 13 said no thanks you're a lardo queen.

The Guard said if you walk through the Garden of Life,
She will automatically become your wife.
Pharto 13 asked if he could see out of his one eye socket?
Because you are about to see the fastest rocket.
They started the engines as fast as they could spin it.
Cause the brats helped the crew phart at the same minute.

They were traveling faster than a meteor,
Almost faster than the brats heater.
They flew past the sun and the moon,
They landed on the rocky Neptune.
Once there they met with an alien,
She told them her name was Sabian.

The aliens believed in interbreeding and had some kids,
They were funny looking without mouths and eyelids.
They told the crew and brats all they wanted was a way to go out,
The crew had to think of something as there was no doubt.
As the crew pharted their way into the night,
The aliens were never again within their sight.

Frank A. Pellegrino

A NEVER ENDING TRIP

The skies looked cold and gray,
Pharto Fourteen was coming our way.
The crew was heading for the sun,
Just to phart and have some fun.
Their pharts smelled like rotten cabbage,
With this stench the crew wasn't sure they could manage.

They all laughed but found out it wasn't really a joke,
When one by one, they all began to choke.
All of a sudden all their hopes were dashed,
Because suddenly the Pharto Fourteen rocket crashed.
The crew discovered they had crashed on Planet No-Phart,
Also Pharto 14 rocket would not start.

The crew and the brats were told they would have to stay alive,
Until another Pharto hopefully would soon arrive.
The next day they all pharted together,
They blasted their way from sun and dreary weather.
They landed in a thick of some Jungle,
When all of a sudden they heard pygmies mumble.

The pygmies served the brats and crew Zebra soup,
The brats swore up and down it tasted like poop.
The brats went over by a big tree to puke,
The powerful puke killed the tree's roots.
Once again they all pharted and pharted and flew to Mars,
To their surprise they saw the Rover there with a car.

An intelligent Martian put the brats in the car and put them in a Zoo,
No expeditions left for the Pharto crew.
The brats escaped during the night,
They were so scared they went far away out of sight.
They fell in the sky and were going from star to star,
They were looking forever for that Pharto type car.

All at once they were hit by a cyclone,
Somehow they landed close by here at home.
You will be hearing about the brats real soon,
If they can survive the Pharto Fumes.

THE PHARTO LUNATIC

Driving by near the warm ocean,
They heard a loud vibrating explosion.
They looked in the direction of the Maple trees,
The explosive force bared all the tree's leaves.
Where they were was a huge mound,
Also a large hole in the ground.

In the air was the largest rocket the brats had ever seen,
To their surprise it was Pharto Fifteen.
It was speeding and the motor was like a stutter,
Flying through the clouds like it was cutting butter.
It was then they pharted their gas,
They all could see a lot of shattering glass.

Flying through the clouds and rain,
Pharto 15 was either drunk or had gone insane.
Captain Pharto flipping his remote control,
The crew landed and started their foot patrol.
While walking the crew were all singing a tune,
This when they spotted a man in the moon.

How long he had been there they didn't know,
Captain Pharto said this man was not taken there by a UFO.
They could tell this man came from America,
But wondered why his headquarters was in the Antarctica,
This man soon ran out of gas with garlic and peppers,
Even with his skunk cabbage used as a helper.

Captain Pharto questioned this man to see if he was sane,
The man told him that he was once wired in his brain.
Pharto Gas is sickening to say the least,
Sickening enough to kill man or beast.
The poor man's mind apparently snapped,
His appointment was over when the Psychiatrist's hand clapped.

Frank A. Pellegrino

BEAUTY HEAVEN AND PEACE

Rocket Pharto Sweet Sixteen just left the refueling station,
With a crew of 16 they flew over the United Nations.
They flew over the New York Yankee Stadium,
Dropping off in aid, soaked Yankee baseballs filled with radium.
The crew had to get together and they pharted va … va …. va…voom,
Off they blasted straight for the moon.
They landed in a field that was full of sheep,
They were tended by one awesome looking creep.

Pharto 16 pharted one more big spray,
Lo and behold the sheep ran away.
The crew with the brats walked through the soggy sheep dip,
They awkwardly fell into it as far up as their lips.
The crew took the poop and dried it in the sun like art,
They made a drug that they later called Phart.
They all were drugged for a very long week,
Soon they pharted away from this creek.

They all flew away to an unknown Planet called Ethanol,
They realized if they strike a match this would be the end of it all.
They had created a mixture of Ethanol and Glycerin,
Topped with sweet potatoes, pharto balls and Listerine.
When lit it would be very shocking,
For it would render one brat deaf and 2 other brats rocking.

They learned some information that made them afraid,
So they flew into space and began to fade.
They landed on another unknown Planet again,
This was a planet of beautiful women and no men.
The women were pretty and had wonderful attitudes,
The crew said the best part of all is these women were nude.

An announcement was made that all flying would automatically cease,
Because Pharto Sixteen had finally found peace.
With so much beauty Pharto 16 said who needs TV?
For Pharto 16, with the brats and his crew, you will never again see.

SEVENTEEN HOT PHARTS

Once upon a time someone like the brats found a bomb quite round,
They said just imagine if it exploded if it would make a loud sound.
They were told to lift the bomb and put it into a large yellow cab,
The cab drove the brats to an experimental lab.
At the lab they put together a high explosive,
The bomb looked like a large locomotive.

So Captain Pharto said attach the bomb to the Pharto Rocket,
The crew with the brats strained and pharted and pharted.
The Pharto Rocket took off so fast from its mound,
Somehow the take off left the rocket wheels on the ground.
When the whole crew realized they had departed,
They told the brats it was their blasto pharts that got them started.

They landed on the Moon and then went on to Mars,
They scouted around looking for Grandpa Franco star after star.
Everything went smoothly till the big ole bomb exploded,
All of the Pharto Seventeen crew got their pants loaded.
They began parachuting one by one and landed on their feet,
They all landed in horse manure that was two feet deep.

Right away they began to radio some emergency calls,
They even radioed the 914th Airborne in Niagara Falls.
The crew was told this planet was called Phart-a-Lot,
The base told them they were not sure if they could find them or not.
Finally a new rocket arrived from over the border,
The rocket from Washington brought the crew new orders.

Since they flew off course they were sent to Iraq,
Once in Iraq they were ordered to help fight off attacks.
The brats were scared and hid in their cages while the crew did their part,
By killing the enemy they used the brats and crews many pharts.
They all ate some hot peppers and pharted steaming hot,
They arrived back home in a Pharting Sling Shot.

Frank A. Pellegrino

PHARTO EIGHTEEN GETS LOST IN SPACE

They all said it was an unbelievable scene,
The brats told Captain Pharto this is like an artist's dream.
The camera indicated there were seeing parachuting balloons,
The men were approaching one of Mar's moons.
Pharto Eighteen soon hit the ground,
The rocket hit the ground, pound after pound.

The rocket weighed a lot like a ship of cargo,
Each piece of cargo had a nickname and it was Lardo.
Pharto Eighteen had done a lot of traveling,
He said it was time to do some unraveling.
They didn't think there was much of anything living there,
Pharto Eighteen and his crew didn't scout around or even care.

Pharto Eighteen disappeared into the night,
They sped so fast before anyone knew it they were out of sight.
They landed on an unknown plant called Heat,
All anyone could see was flowers and they smelled so sweet.
The brats thought they were in a dreamland or even paradise,
Perhaps this was a Flower Planet and had not realized.

Before they knew it the whole crew together sneezed,
There was an arousing of baseball size bees.
Eighteen Lardos crammed into the rocket of Pharto Eighteen,
They all pharted together and caused a giant smoke screen.
Once again they pharted together and surprisingly disappeared,
They flew far off into a big smoky hemisphere.

Soon they landed after a long rough ride,
They had landed on the Moon's rocky dark side.
Here they saw very tall stonewalls,
One crew member said it is a look-a-like, Niagara Falls.
They met a lot of short people and they had big heads,
The majority of the short people had hair that was the color of red.
After saying good night to the short people the crew hit the love sack,
The whole crew and brats swore together this is one place we will never go back.

CHAPTER VI

ALIEN BEAUTIES AND THE BRATS

UFO ANGELS APPEAR

One sunny day near the ocean,
The brats were starting to apply body lotion.
To their surprise a UFO, came from the ocean floor,
A beautiful Angel opened her door.

She told the brats that her name was LOVE,
She had been sent there from above.
She said she came form a planet called Drolly,
This is a religious planet most Holy.

The Angel said, she was sent there by her leader,
He is a 'planet advisor' called Peter.
Peter advises all of the aliens that are dangerous strangers,
He places us in the midst of all kinds of dangers.

She told the brats what is really, really worse,
Is these dangerous strangers want to capture the universe.
The brats looking frightened, the Angel told them don't be too alarmed,
For she was sent to them to keep them from being harmed.

The Angel also said a strong voice will call you from the sky,
Pray, and He will spare you, no one will die.
So even if you have been bad or have sinned,
Remember, if in God you do believe, you will be forgiven by Him.

The brats told this Angel she reminded them of their poor Granny,
Granny always told us that no prayer was too many.
They also said Granny told them prayers will always succeed;
We just have to be truthful and in God believe.

Frank A. Pellegrino

UFO ALIEN ANGELS

Remember Captain Pharto said if you ever see a UFO.
They might not always be our foe.
Some of the occupants are of another civilization,
Some of them are from another of God's creations.

Bonnie asked are they checking our population?
Do you think they are checking the defenses of our nation?
Ingrid asked why is it whenever the aliens appear,
All the cattle up here seem to disappear?

Captain Pharto said maybe they are looking for seed,
Or perhaps for a special mix breed.
You know they have abducted people before,
Like last time, they will do it more and more.

Captain Pharto also said they come from beyond the ozone,
They come from Heaven or from Planets yet unknown.
Remember these aliens have skin of green,
For some reason they are seldom seen.

Captain Pharto reminded the brats even though they seem to be strangers,
It has also been proved that some of them are God's Angels.
You brats should be very good and start to prepare,
As I have forewarned you and made you hopefully aware.

Bonnie said maybe the UFO Angels would take us to our Lord,
And finally we could receive our just rewards.
Ingrid added no matter what Granny thinks is bad behavior,
She too will know we will be welcomed home by our Savior.

FLYING SAUCER FRIENDS

Captain Pharto said people have seen UFO's for centuries,
They visit planets and many countries,
They are often surrounded by flashes of light,
He told the brats this is a beautiful sight to see at night.

Flying saucer aliens are usually good friends,
But be careful as some are good, some bad, it all depends.
When flying saucers move away or to the ground,
They will speed away without a sound.

Captain Pharto said he found it is best to show them good cheer,
Instead of being rude or full of fear.
Some people have been taken aboard and anesthetized,
Then the aliens let them go when they become hypnotized.

Some authorities want you to forget what you saw,
Even though you are not breaking the law.
Be careful as the odd looking aliens may be strangers,
They could be Guardian Angels seeing danger.

Brenda asked are they here to help us from evil?
Before this coming earth upheaval!
She cried out God is alive and real,
I know in my heart only God can heal.

You brats should have thought about this when you were being bad,
Playing with sticks and bricks and making your Granny so mad.
He told them they had better reinforce their faith,
Before one of these aliens takes them to God's Pearly Gates.

Frank A. Pellegrino

A SPACE BEAUTY

The two brats sent Brenda a UFO letter and said the female must have come from Venus,
Because that female you met is the prettiest up here amongst us.
Here she stands up straight and looks about six feet,
She cleaned us up and we are all dressed so clean and neat.

She has long blond hair running down to her hips,
Remember her flashing blue eyes and ruby red lips?
She admitted she came from a Planet called Rainbow,
They told Brenda behind them was a flashing orange UFO.

Would you believe she left for this voyage at age twenty?
Now she is thin and weak but a young looking seventy.
Up here we can push a button and disappear,
Push the button again and reappear.

She told us Earth was just a baby,
We can hardly believe she is a seventy year old lady.
She is leaving and can't take us with her she said,
Before you would reach my Planet, you would be dead.

With a speedy, soundless and unreal burst,
The female you met flew out in the endless Universe.
Please tell Captain Pharto this is not a dream,
We are begging to rejoin Captain Pharto's space team.

UFO's ARE EVERYWHERE

Captain Pharto told Brenda we all see the shining distant stars,
They are just as bright as the Planet Mars.
He said he knew at one time Mars had people living there,
Also there were rivers and lakes everywhere.

He told Brenda they had mountains, plants and trees,
Even dinosaurs, elephants, birds and stinging bees.
These inhuman people were ahead of our time,
Who knows they could be yours or maybe ancestors of mine.

Brenda worrying about Bonnie and Ingrid asked where did UFO's originate?
She said I hear tell where they like to congregate.
Captain Pharto said on the moon's many craters,
Most live where life was built by spacemen's creators.

Some tell us there is evidence the aliens came from Venus,
For sure, they are too far ahead of us.
News of flying UFO's made the aliens a sensation,
They keep an ongoing curiosity of people's imagination.

Captain Pharto said Earth also has their amount of UFO's;
Remember both ends of Earth are two large holes.
Brenda fretting about her sister brats, asked, can you find UFO's here?
Sure Captain Pharto told her, just keep looking into our atmosphere.

Frank A. Pellegrino

UNKNOWN ALIENS

The brats met some people from outer space,
They could tell they were of an unknown race.
Brenda said they don't look like me, or you,
She said, my, oh my, their skin looks like a royal blue.

They saw a female who looked thin and weak,
She approached the brats and kissed each on their cheeks.
Ingrid thought she could be a celebrity,
As the female spoke to her through mental telepathy.

Bonnie said she is very short and has shapely hips,
She has very large ears and ruby red lips.
The female told the brats her planet has a need,
She was sent there for a reason and they wanted her to interbreed.

She also told the brats her off springs would be white and blue,
Hopefully the off springs would have a sprinkle of red too.
She said she was looking for some American mates,
Her off springs would always bless the United States.

She pointed at Ingrid and Bonnie, then to the sky,
She told Ingrid and Bonnie to pack up, for today they will soon fly.
She said we will fly past the distant Planet Mars,
Leaving Brenda alone as they flew far into the Universe past the stars.

ALIENS FROM WITHIN

Captain Pharto said there are Aliens in outer space,
Also there are aliens starring you right now in your face.
Every day they like to rub shoulder everywhere,
Take notice sometimes they travel in pairs.

Is it true they come from beyond the North Pole?
Captain Pharto said they are tall giants from the hollow Earth hole.
Bonnie asked are these giants similar to humans?
Captain said yes and some are robots or simply inhuman.

Captain Pharto told the brats certain scientists traveling with the expeditionary forces,
Were approached and these in human's stilled the scientist's voices.
Ingrid asked why was the information censored about Antarctica?
She also asked why was this information struck out in America?

The brats wanted to know how long have these creatures been here?
Do you think they are the ones polluting our atmosphere?
They also asked have they harnessed the powers of the pyramid?
Or have they perfected human and inhuman hybrid?

Captain Pharto said the discovery of the hallow Earth is a mystery,
Making this news public will make world history.
He told the scared brats if you rub shoulders with a stranger,
Pay attention and remember you could be facing danger.

Frank A. Pellegrino

ALIEN ADVICE

The Aliens said they really didn't plan it,
But told the brats they came from another planet.
They said they came here to explore,
So they are going to the mushroom houses questioning door to door.

The Aliens have been all over this turf,
Asking what has happened to the beautiful Earth?
They told the brats you have had W.W.I and W.W. II,
Additional wars since and now the Iraq War too.

The World has scarred Mother Earth's face,
Fighting all over the Middle East has been a disgrace.
The Aliens said they were not college professors,
It doesn't take a bright professor to know who are the aggressors.

Brenda said I believe the aggressor is Bin-Laden,
In her eyes he is the mark of the beast Satan.
The Alien replied, Bin-Laden ordered a plane to crash on us,
But we retaliated and now there is no fuss.

The Aliens said we shouldn't blast Earth piece by piece,
You brats need to try living on Earth with Peace.
The Aliens went on to say we have to report to their Planet where it is cold,
But told the brats, here is a reminder to you, Peace is worth more than gold.

A CRAZY DREAM

Bonnie said once she was just another unknown,
But never again will she ever be alone.
She said she wouldn't ever again wait for the tone,
On her old dusty telephone.
She said she met a handsome man on this train,
Captain Alien was his name.

She fell in love ever so deep,
Now she can't rest or even sleep.
She said they made love in the dark,
She could hear the thumping of her heart.
They embraced and kissed and kissed,
They were making up for all the time they had missed.

All of a sudden she heard her parent's voices,
They were telling her she had no choices.
They told her there would be a huge thunderbolt,
A big one too, like a powerful ten thousand volt.
Then out of no where came a an orange glow,
Lo and Behold it was a huge roaring UFO.

Oh No, never again would she see his face,
Because he had to return to outer space.
Bonnie thought he had been telling her lies,
He hypnotized her mind and she felt paralyzed.
The next UFO explosion was like lightning,
This was scary and very frightening.

The UFO flew away in thick black smoke,
Thank God Bonnie finally awoke.
She was screaming and crying at the same time,
Captain Pharto told her this is what happens when one doesn't mind.

Frank A. Pellegrino

UFO's FLY HIGH AND LOW

Captain Pharto said look there are UFO's in the sky day and night,
He said most of the time they are beyond sight.
Sometimes they fly in squads and tonight there is only one,
The brats said where in the world do they come from.

They often land quickly on the ground,
Hardly do they make a humming sound.
Captain Pharto said sometimes they come in a fireball,
The UFO. will try to contact us with a signal call.

Far out in the blue sky and outer space,
Captain Pharto said they could easily out speed any one of us in a race.
Brenda said do you think the Government knows all about them?
She said they didn't look like the little green men.

The brats said they hoped their contact would increase,
Perhaps they could show us the way to world peace.
Scared Ingrid said she hoped they were not people eaters,
Or not those one-eyed ugly creatures.

Bonnie said I think I saw one when we were in the Milky Way,
If they were Aliens or Angels, she really couldn't say.
Captain Pharto told them things could change for better or worse,
He said this is an unbelievable vast universe.

In the future, Captain Pharto said you brats will see more and more,
The Alien presence you should not ignore.
Maybe they are infertile and can't recreate,
But like most Aliens, they are looking for good mates.

IS IT TRUE?

The brats watched as she came from the brightest star,
Far, far beyond the planet Mars.
They said she had an aura on her head,
But it was her real beauty instead.

Describing her they said she was five feet two,
Her eyes were a beautiful sky blue.
She was wearing a wide belt with sparkling stones,
So bright it could pierce their bodies and tingle their bones.

She told them she came from a planet far away,
Also she was very tired and told them she would like a long stay.
She had a walk like she was stepping on eggs,
Because she walked without bending her legs.

She told the brats she wanted to teach this generation,
Something about secret science of levitation.
She also wanted to teach them about gravity,
The brats looked at each other and said this is enough to cause insanity.

To the brats surprise she told them she wanted them to interbreed,
She had twenty women ready to receive the first seed.
Afterwards she would take them back to their planet ZO,
Flying in their silver colored UFO.

The next moment was frightening,
The UFO. was hit by lightning.
The vibrating noises were very loud,
And the twenty beauties faded into the crowd.

When the brats told Captain Pharto about this episode,
He was upset and scolded them for telling such a story so bold.
He said you cannot prove any of this you claim to have seen,
Because in reality, this is a fantasy, and he was sure it was only a dream.

Frank A. Pellegrino

CHAPTER VII

CAPTAIN PHARTO AND THE

END OF THE PHARTOS

PHARTO TWENTY CALLED TO THE RESCUE

Pharto Nineteen and his crew went to look for Pharto Eighteen,
They searched and searched on the computer and TV screens.
They traveled through unbelievable distances,
They encountered no enemies nor Alien resistance.
They finally hit the ground and the rocket parked,
Phew! Said Pharto Nineteen, the air smells like Pharto pharts.

Pharton Nineteen knew that Pharto Eighteen had to be close by,
The smell was strong and powerful enough to make them die.
Captain Pharto 1Nineteen shouted to his crew, let's be quiet and listen,
Very soon out of a cave came a crowd of children.
The children said this is the Moon,
They had been dropped off blindfolded by someone from Neptune.

Pharto Nineteen knew they had to be from their parents of the U.S.A.,
He saw by a large crater an American Flag on display.
The children said they felt healthy but without any meat,
They were eating Moon bananas but mostly vegetables they had to eat.
The children said they got their Vitamin D from the sun,
Vitamin C they were getting from the Moon and then some.

It was starting to get cold and very late,
So the crew went to their rocket to fumigate.
It was shocking and quite a surprise when the rocket wouldn't start,
Pharto Nineteen got his crew together and they couldn't phart.
Pharto Nineteen told his crew and the brats, I guess the next thing on our menu,
Is to wait for Pharto Twenty to come to our rescue.

Pharto Nineteen said Pharto Twenty would be shaped like a wing,
He told the scared brats that this rocket could speed pass anything.
This new Pharto Twenty could and would spout Phart, Phart,
Pharto Twenty was built to be a rescuing transport,
Pharto Nineteen told everyone they would be back sometime this century,
In the meantime, don't forget the rocket Pharto Twenty.

Frank A. Pellegrino

PHARTO BLASTO PLANET

While waiting on Pharto Twenty they all thought they would fall apart,
They kept hearing jokes about this Phart and that Phart.
They all laughed so hard they feared they would crush their hearts,
When they heard a brat say a gentleman told her she was the only one smart.

They all laughed so hard and to their knees they fell,
Because a new aroma came over them that didn't smell well.
It was like going down a crowded elevator with a big blast,
To the crew's surprise there came a blast and a powerful gas.

The crew and brats were reeling all about,
One by one, the crew and brats all passed out.
The rocket elevator suddenly stopped,
Just one person in the elevator had not dropped.

A pump was used on everyone by the rocket hospital crew,
The blast had broken everything and the oxygen tanks blew.
Out of nowhere came some women in a carriage,
The horrible blast had caused many of the women to miscarriage.

A new crew came from somewhere wearing gas masks,
They said what a deadly stench and what a task.
What these people need is to eat some BEANO,
Soon after wash it down with some good VINO.

It wasn't the fault of the Mexican beans after all,
Pharto 19 thought sure this is what caused them to faint and fall.
He learned the beans came from the Planet Blasto,
He told everyone this was their sister Planet of Pharto.

NO NEEDFOR CONSTIPATION PROBLEMS

Captain Pharto said there is no bigger helper,
If you brats will remember to eat a red hot pepper.
Bear in mind, when you need or want to go to the John afterwards,
Expect everyone you know to be waiting in line and this is absurd.

If you find you are suffering from constipation,
Don't force yourself as this could cause a big abrasion.
Just relax and don't let go with lots of emotion,
If you do it will cause a fiery and volcanic explosion.

Eating big red hot peppers will play a big part,
You will not endure constipation, but just a big Phart!
Some hot peppers you might want to avoid,
Because the explosive force could knock out your hemorrhoids.

Now if you decide to take a dose of castor oil,
Remember this will cause your innards to boil.
You might want to take water pills and be the wiser,
Because water pills will work like a geyser.

Red Hot Peppers will cause a stomach inferno for sure,
Sorry brats there just isn't any better cure.
But if you decide to take EX-LAX,
Please, Please, don't you dare try to relax.

One thing more Captain Pharto said, you may get the runs,
Some of his crew got them ton after ton.
Sometimes he said Constipation often makes him wonder,
Perhaps it would be better to just use a toilet plunger.

Frank A. Pellegrino

SECRET GAS WEAPON

The brats began to tell their story how beans are an explosive issue,
They said gas eventually will injure all your bodies tissues.
It also means a person that is shaped like a jelly bean,
Will act like a Mexican jumping bean it seems.

When you are on a bus, whatever it is, don't ask,
Just open your purse and put on a mask.
If your vision seems to become blurred,
Most likely it will be hard to be endured.

They were asked does gas have lasting effect?
Does it have any effect on sex?
They replied, you look like you have been battered,
Your face will pale and if you wear glasses they will be shattered.

They said some people have high speed gas,
Enough gas to break your living room glass.
Some of the high octane gases, human gas, will deafen,
The brats said it should be made into a war weapon.

The brats said sometimes beans tend to explode,
Sometimes it will cause one to leave behind a big load.
They said beans are supposed to be nutritious,
They are very healthy and delicious.

They continued to say that beans have proven to be strong as dynamite,
One continuous big blast will cause one to lose their appetite.
They said if you do choose to eat beans don't pass the gas on,
Please do your best to smother it by sitting on your John.

PHARTS OF THE ARTS

The brats said don't ever underestimate the power of the bean,
It has been known to us to blast away sometimes your spleen.
It could even happen in the middle of your dream,
Then be sure to check when you wake if your sheets are clean.
They said the more powerful one is known as Pharto Scene,
It is also known as Pharto Supreme.

They said if in doubt, just ask two-ton Josephine,
Her aroma has a smell like Pharts and Kerosene.
Be sure to look into all your children's jeans,
Their pharts may have molded into the color green.
When you begin to smell some smelly cream,
Remember it is bean power from your teens.

There is another powerful Pharto Vaseline,
It is called we were told Pharto Kerosene.
Pharto bean gas is called Pharto Gasoline,
We were told it is a mixture of gasoline and tangerines.
We saw two women having a phart war and one named Doreen,
Doreen's so powerful she knocked down her friend, Geraldine.

A pharto bean mixture is part fossilgene,
This is more powerful than strychnine.
The brats went on to say that putting all these phart beans together is a pity,
They said it truly could flatten out New York City.
They said the more beans you eat, the more they stream,
They said trust us they smell a whole lot worse than it seems,

These Pharto Pharts are definitely carried to an extreme,
They fill the universal air and could plug up a computer screen.
These pharts are dangerous and say what they mean,
They are skunky enough that they would embarrass the British Queen.

Frank A. Pellegrino

RESPONSE TO AN OLD PHART

Granny thinks pharting is a state of the art,
That is why she told Captain Pharto to teach the brats the power of a phart.
Captain Pharto said it is so easy to just let it pass,
We brats told him it is too bad we can't 'can' this smelly gas.

He said did you ever hear of laughing gas you lasses?
You should feel much relief by just letting it pass.
We laughed so hard when it passed in our pants,
But we found out later we had our pants full of ants.

He told us it would make the Earth dark soon,
If we let our cheesy pharts cover the Moon.
With all the power and stink that our pharts make us heave,
It was enough to blow away the Maple tree leaves.

Sometimes Captain Pharto smelled of gas fumes,
But other times he smelled like our sweet perfume.
Sometimes whether a phart is from woman or man,
Be careful when it is directed towards a fan.

Sometimes it is a phart that causes you to awake,
Even though it will often sound like a big earthquake.
After so much pharting both day and night,
This may be the reason so many people's hair turns white.

Perhaps we should give the pharting business the big AX,
The brats told Captain Pharto they would rather take EX-LAX.
One thing for sure pharts don't smell like a tasty stew,
Here the brats go again, Phew, Phew Phew!

[Captain Pharto's motto is: It is better to bare the shame than to bare the pain]

DO YOU KNOW STINKO?

The brats said sometimes it is very hard to tell,
Exactly what that odor is that everyone smells.
Sometimes they said it smells so bad,
It not only overwhelms them but it also makes them mad.

Sometimes the odor smells like sewer fumes,
Other times it smells like ten cents a gallon perfume.
Sometimes it smells like rancid sauerkraut,
The smell is strong enough to make all of them pass out.

The brats went on to say that some smells were like rotten fish,
Smelled so bad that wishing death would be your number one wish.
Some crew pharts smelled like real strong cologne,
Now the brats realized why the crew was always alone.

Sometimes they could smell what they thought was Chanel Number Five,
But not true long enough and they were lucky to come out alive.
Heaven help us if we smelled a skunk,
The skunk stench often came from someone drunk.

Captain Pharto told us to be careful and not get caught in the rocket elevator,
When they picked up hippies and aliens they smelled like an alligator.
If it was a sulphur like stench it probably came from the brats pets,
This stench was a paralyzing odor no one would forget.

Frank A. Pellegrino

PHARTS AND FARTS

This old Phart, with his dart,
Shoots arrow Pharts with all his heart.
One bounced off a big stone,
The phart hit Bonnie's funny bone.

At the end of each Pharty day,
Pharts will pile high as a stack of hay.
As the pharts age they will mature,
Smelling like cow and horse manures.

It's so rotten and it smells,
It gets into the human cells.
But when it smells like elephant dung,
It will fill up your lungs and you die young.

When it hardens you can make a chain,
Maybe for Bonnie the brat, she will make a cane.
If it doesn't work, don't complain,
The incorrigible brats won't lose or gain.

Captain Pharto keeps the brats busy,
He doesn't want them to be just smelly sissys.
He has a name for all their stinking pharts,
A name is listed on their cages every time they fart.

CAPAIN PHARTO'S MOTTO: MORE BEANS PLEASE

Captain Pharto would ask have you indulged in your pork and beans?
He would say, if not, let me explain what this will mean.

First it means dodging dangerous and thunderous bullets,
The pharts from the pork and beans does its job to the fullest.

Eating more proteins will help you gather more steam,
The thunderous bullets will make you want to scream.

Eating pork and beans will make you nice and lean,
Because they are heavily loaded with high protein.

Sometimes they sound like major thunderstorms,
When the pharts start coming they come in many forms.

He told the brats to protect their precious pets,
He also advised them to wear a constructioner's helmet.

All the above mentioned by Captain Pharto is true,
He told the brats this above advice should help you.

The pharts at last will give you a lot of free liberty,
If not, Captain Pharto said here is my sympathy.

Frank A. Pellegrino

SPACE IN THE UNIVERSE

Captain Pharto told the brats whatever country lands first on Mars,
Will harness all the Global World's powers.
He said it will be rewarding and quite astounding,
But quite sure it will take months before any landing.
Captain Pharto told the brats to beware of any human forms,
These human forms would cause rainy weather and electrical storms.

He said he hopes the brats can find a lot of H2o,
Perhaps they might even see lots of white snow.
If not, they will have to deal with sun dried rivers and lakes,
Plus a lot of red dust these electrical storms will make.
Captain Pharto said he knows there is water somewhere hidden out of sight,
He told the brats they would find hidden below ground shadows of the night.

Since this is the year that they all landed there,
The brats wanted to take pictures everywhere.
They argued about finding an Army of UFO.,
But worried if underground the temperatures would be below zero.
Captain Pharto predicts that in the future and probably soon,
Americans will be establishing settlements all over the Moon.

Captain Pharto said they would not be seeing little green men around,
Most of them now live in the craters deep into the ground.
The brats laughed and said Captain Pharto is telling us half truths,
But Captain Pharto said he would show them the real proof.
Inter-planet life for the brats would become a curse,
As living on the Moon is a never ending space in the universe.

A SPACE NIGHTMARE

As Captain Pharto looked into his trusty old Crystal Ball,
He saw the stars, the universe and said I have seen it all.
They all were at an experimental military station,
He pushed a button and they all blew out into Creation.

It pushed them to the upper layers of light air,
They didn't even have a flight suit to wear.
They were about to fly through falling snow,
Suddenly they were picked up by an enormous UFO.

The green eyed Alien was bald, tall and walked like he was made of JELLO,
The brats said he seemed polite, gentle spoken and a tall gentle fellow.
The Alien flew them to Mars, Pluto and Neptune,
The Alien said their last destination would be the Moon.

Captain Pharto told the brats they would be shocked to see an American settlement,
Also if they didn't start behaving this was going to be their stay permanent.
They were all protected by atmospheric storms,
As their assignments were making permanent air space platforms.

The brats were told they could never leave,
Also they would be meeting lots of Adam and Eves.
They were told from the beginning of human birth.
The Moon was once part of the Earth.

They were all shown a big patch of giant mushrooms,
Each mushroom was actually a house with five rooms.
Around each house were factories making UFO parts,
These factories were put together and shaped like darts.

Captain Pharto told the Alien if the brats were good, they could return someday,
But he made the Alien promise he would land them back in the U.S.A.
Captain Pharto told the Alien to please teach these brats how to live in Peace,
So they could spread the word back home how to make wars cease.

Frank A. Pellegrino

FROM ANOTHER PLANET

The brats said they saw a man seven feet tall,
He was trying to play with Ingrid the sport of football.
When he would run after Ingrid he would make the ground shake,
Tackling her, she felt like her bones would break.

Bonnie and Brenda said he was so ugly, ugly as sin,
They both said he had a half-moon shaped chin.
He had a six inch nose and sexy crossed eyes,
But Ingrid didn't think he was the ugliest of guys.

The brats didn't want to get his attention,
All that this man eats they didn't want to mention.
His brains? Well the brats said he had some,
But Ingrid would not tell what Planet he came from.

The brats said he actually had no brains,
For sure he had no feelings, no gains or pains.
Before Ingrid he couldn't find a mate,
He couldn't even find a gal for a date.

He said he could no longer stand it,
He was taking Ingrid and going back to his Planet.
They took a flight on a UFO,
Where they went no one seems to know.

Captain Pharto found him later with a broken neck,
They had been in an accident, because the UFO had wrecked.
Ingrid told Captain Pharto this accident was all about him and his glory,
But Captain Pharto said to Ingrid, this is not the end of your story.

DREAMS AND MORE DREAMS

On a cold, chilly, dark night,
The brats looked out the window at a bright light.
It was a multi-colored flash and swish,
For some reason it quickly seemed to just vanish.

There was a frenzy noise of loud drums,
Strong enough to burst the brat's eardrums.
The brats saw dancing and sprinkling of magic powder,
There was lots of singing and the drums grew louder.

The brats realized these people were witches,
The witches singing left the brats in stitches.
The brats asked these people what are you doing here?
The replied they were from a different atmosphere.

They said they noticed Earth's wars are on the increase,
While their planet knows only Peace.
They said God gave us a Heaven with Peace in mind,
They were here to help people of all colors wherever they could find.

They told the brats the name of their Planet is MO
They arrived here in a flashing UFO.
They also said it is now time for them to get ready to leave,
One more thing to remember, they had one wish each and they would now receive.

The brats saw a flash and a thundering roar,
And to their surprise they fell out of bed to the floor.
The three brats laughed till they were bursting at the seams,
Realizing all of Granny's disciplines were causing them to have these dreams.

Frank A. Pellegrino

THE END OF THE PHARTOS

Pharto Twenty rocket pilot named Freddy,
Had high alert orders to hurry and get ready.
He was told to use a highly secret formula blast,
The crew had to all together pass a lot of gas.
They pharted so hard it caused a big strain,
The pharts started a fire in huge field of sugar cane.

After receiving a distress signal they had to be sent,
On the way to the Moon they blasted and went.
First they landed on a large field farm,
Someone directed them to a big red barn.
Here they captured a group of Aliens,
Amongst them was a group of beautiful female Australians.

The females were so beautiful and adoring,
They wanted to help and began pharting as the rocket was exploring.
Phart after Phart they soon were pharting out flames,
Some pharts so hard they began to have real pains.
On this rocket there was room a plenty,
This rocket so big it could seat one hundred and seventy.

When they were all seated Pilot Freddy took the lead,
He said everyone phart together as we need to make a new Phart Breed.
There were children aboard who were hybrids,
One brat said the people all look the same, even the kids.
Whenever they ate, it was a plateful of cucumbers,
This created a lot of gas and sounded like thunder.

The strong pharts clouded the air and clouded the view,
Pilot Freddy had everyone locked up in the rocket cages like in a Zoo.
They kept pharting as they crossed a big field leading to a gas station,
The horrible pharts blew up everything in the creation.
The brats were left for later return as all the Phartos were ordered to retire,
The Government said Captain Pharto would remain but for now there will be no new rehires.

BACK TO EARTH

A UFO. speeding the fastest speed ever seen,
Behind the UFO was the longest and darkest smoke screen.
The stench was strong enough to blow the brats new hair away,
The stench had come from the direction of the Milky Way.

The UFO would burn the grass on the ground,
It was flying in the cow pastures and not making any sounds.
The little green men came out wearing their backpacks,
They were also wearing their gas masks.

The UFO team had their own gas station,
They had enough gas to stink out the whole nation.
The name of the gas or stinks was called Phart,
It stunk so bad it could knock one out of a cart.

They told the brats they hope no one has a bad heart,
The brats said they should rename their gas "State of the Art".
For the next meal they were served none other than beans,
They ate so much that the uniforms they were wearing split at the seams.

The brats were told wearing their gas masks would not hurt,
Much to their surprise the gas masks did not work.
The brats woke up in the middle of next week,
They were sick, had diaherra and feeling very weak.

The brats were told they were in a Planet past the Moon,
That they would be sent home very soon.
The Aliens all pharted at the same time,
The brats landed back on Earth somewhere, each on their behind.

Frank A. Pellegrino

CAPTAIN PHARTO AND CREW REST IN PEACE

This rocket is the fastest one under the sun,
It is the fastest most powerful rocket second to none.
It was named Pharto Phart Beans
The largest Pharto Rocket ever seen.

It can fly a thousand times around the Earth with a glass of fuel,
Flying farther with a mixture of skunk and dog stool.
This rocket is so powerful it could tarnish your ring,
The crew pharts on this rocket were really something.

The rocket flew around and around the brightest stars,
Before they finally landed on the Planet Mars.
The crew met with some green pygmies,
One brat said they were about three feet shorter than me.

You could tell these creatures were suffering from hunger,
They had noses that looked like a toilet plunger.
The pygmies were powerful swimmers from the lakes,
They swam with their ears that looked like pancakes.

The pygmies asked if Captain Pharto would take them to the Moon,
Pharto Phart Bean told the Captain there just was not enough room.
To the amazement of the crew and brats Pharto Phart Bean pharted in the pygmies eyes,
Then he flew the rocket far away into the skies.

The crew began to drink a very strong potion,
Causing the pilot and crew to crash into the ocean.
The brats said please God send a new crew,
Could it be a blessing for them and Granny too?

This had been the first time a Pharto Rocket had totally failed,
While the brats wait for Granny and crew they will be sleeping with a Pharto Whale.
The brats were dreaming as they slept with the Pharto Whale,
They prayed to God and said they would be good as this discipline had been hell.

THE END OF THE SEQUEL

ABOUT THE AUTHOR

Aliceanne Pellegrino-Henricks was born in Bloomington, Indiana and lived there until 2001 when she married Frank A Pellegrino and moved to Niagara Falls, New York.

After her late husband's death in 2006, She remarried George B. Henricks in 2009 on Valentine's Day. A beautiful life of love and togetherness makes for their happy marriage.

The author is a mother of two children, Tim L. Gilmore and Marianne Gilmore, Jordan. Both children gave her two Grandsons, Timothy Lewis Gilmore II and Zachary Michael Jordan.

The author here writes about her children, grandchildren and the beauty of life, nature and love. She also likes to write humorous stories. Her late husband, Frank A. Pellegrino had written a book called "The Phartom of the Opera – A Classic of the Gasses" and he always thought a sequel should follow. The author here enjoys writing, playing the piano and organ and being a down to earth housewife. With all the sadness in the world, this author enjoys writing about beautiful things and positive ideas.